Monsters are real, and ghosts are real too.
They live inside us, and sometimes, they win.

Ste[illegible]ing

CURIOUS TALES

OF THE

REGENCY TERRACES

Catherine Page

The Regency Town House

Published by The Regency Town House on behalf of
The Brunswick Town Charitable Trust

Visit our website at www.rth.org.uk

Book and cover design by Alexandra Mckellar

ISBN: 978-1-903709-01-6

For Martin, Sanna and Sam

Foreword

I grew up through the 1960s surrounded by the great terraced houses of Brighton & Hove but it was not until the mid 1980s that I discovered 13 Brunswick Square. Before long I was imagining 'The Regency Town House', a historic home for the City somewhat akin to those found in Bath, York and Edinburgh.

Designed by the Regency architect Charles Augustin Busby, the property was by then divided into flats. Realizing The Regency Town House, as it now exists, has meant reuniting the property's original parts, restoring its defective fabric and, eventually, acquiring the basement of Number 10 three doors to the south; a fabulous 'survivor' that has become 'the servants' annex'.

Today, our volunteers work industriously to progress our varied objectives; some drawing on long-held professional skills such as our architects, carpenters, plasterers and painters. Others develop new competencies in topics such as processing historic data, writing street histories, cataloguing architectural drawings and making clothes.

Annually, we offer house tours, an eclectic assortment of workshops and exhibitions and one of the nation's largest Heritage Open Days programs. With this new book I'm delighted that we are expanding our work as a publisher. What will tomorrow bring!

NICK TYSON

Curator, The Regency Town House

Preface

From the moment I entered the Regency Town House at 13 Brunswick Square, I was intrigued by its history, its otherness and the feeling that under its generous umbrella I would be able to explore my own inner journey – almost wherever that was to lead me. But it wasn't until 2012 that I started to write – how should I put it 'alternative reality' - and that was entirely down to Nushi (Nick Tyson's partner) who said that she had always felt a presence in the kitchen at the back of Number 10's basement and, fixing me with a glare, demanded that I write a ghost story. Reluctant at first, I soon came to appreciate that ghost stories provided a healthy contrast to the fact-based nature of the academic research I was doing at the time and it came as a relief to be able to let my imagination go. Since then, scaring people, just a little at Christmas, has become quite a habit.

Although I was originally inspired by what I knew about Regency society, the area of Brunswick town and some of the people who came to live in its environs, I quickly discovered that the stories could not be held back by everyday reality, although they were often created around a kernel of truth. Over their long history, these houses have been witness to all kinds of vicissitudes of the human spirit and are nothing if not atmospheric. I soon learnt that ghosts cannot be held prisoner either by geography or time.

Initially these stories were meant to be read aloud at our Christmas Entertainments so I have adapted them for the printed page - just a little – with the invaluable help of Bridget Whelan and Jenny Fraser-Smith. Then Jill Vigus joined our team, saw the point of the stories immediately and offered to illustrate them. Special thanks go to Alexandra Mckellar for designing the book and organising the production.

So when the days are dark and short, or the hour of midnight strikes, or a fog is swirling outside, or even when you just want a change of mood, turn off the lamps, light a fire if you can but certainly some candles, and let your imagination go.

Contents

The Curator's Tale

This story is about something that happened one December in the basement of Number 10 Brunswick Square. The housekeeper's room is at the front and with the shutters open, can be quite bright, but as you go down the long corridor to the rear of the basement, any light there is seems to quickly disappear. Even on a good day the wine cellar, the servants' dining room, the yard and, of course, the kitchen at the back of the house are shrouded in stygian gloom. As a researcher who had a few occasions to go down there and investigate, I found that the darkness of the shadows quickly became oppressive. Added to that, the basement was always cold and dank and, over time, it acquired a slightly hostile reputation with those of us who knew it. This was exacerbated by the story I'm going to tell you.

Back in 1994, Nick Tyson, now the Curator, had just acquired the property and he arranged the first public tour of the basement for a Saturday afternoon in early December. The visit was from a children's home and had been set for two o'clock but the coach was late arriving, so it began instead at three o'clock in the gathering winter gloom.

The children were restless and over-excited from the beginning. Very soon they were also extremely cold. They started to dart in and out of unlit rooms and, although Nick tried to make things relevant to them by talking about the lives of children in Regency times, when he finally got to the kitchen the group was on the verge of being out of control. He was about to declare defeat when suddenly there was a piercing scream and a boy ran out of a storeroom at the back of the kitchen. He was white with shock. No amount of reassurance by the kindly staff could get him to say anything about what had scared him. He was incoherent, but his very real fear was obvious to all. In a sober mood, they left.

That evening, Nick received a phone call from the children's home to say the boy had now recovered, but had lost his scarf in the panic. Nick searched the basement all over, checking the darkest corners with a torch, especially the storeroom in the kitchen, but he found nothing.

In the following months the basement became a popular place for tours, but apparently every time children visited the temperature in the kitchen would drop and odd bits of clothing would sometimes disappear. The volunteers at The Regency Town House were regularly deputed to search for missing gloves, scarves and jumpers, but nothing was ever found.

The missing clothes achieved their own mythology and some said they were probably never there in the first place. However, what couldn't so easily be explained was that, time and time again, children who were brave enough to explore the darkest and most obscure store rooms off the kitchen, emerged shaking, shivering and white.

This was too much of a coincidence for me and I became curious and started rooting around, looking for the history of the basement. I found documents that related to the time when the architect, Charles Busby, made an agreement with the local landowner, the Reverend Thomas Scutt, to develop Brunswick Town on his farmland. It seems that in 1824 Scutt evicted a shepherd and his family, not only from his job, but also from his tied cottage. So the shepherd, one William Young, moved his wife and five children to a dank hovel in George Street on the other side of the Steine. He could get no work and died the following year. He was in despair and probably took his own life. His eldest son, Thomas, was just ten years old at this time and, knowing that there was construction work available on the Brunswick Estate, he went back. The records of the firm Cooper & Lynn, who built Number 10, state that a young boy was taken on and, because his hours were so long, he was found a small place to sleep in the basement. I liked to think that the builders took pity on him and brought him food, but it must have been very cold, very lonely and very miserable. This is where all traces of Thomas Young stop. The only clue to his possible fate is that, while building Number 10 there was a catastrophic collapse of the ceiling in the kitchen.

That was as far as I got with the research into the origins of the basement, so I returned to the story that Nick told me.

Because there were so many dark nooks and crannies where people could get lost, it was Nick's policy to count his visitors in and then count them out again as they left. Once the basement front door was locked there was no other way out. It so happened that early one evening whilst showing visitors from another children's home around, he was called away and it was left for someone else to lock up. This person seems not to have been quite as thorough.

Apparently no one noticed until the next day that a boy was missing, but then there was panic. Nervously, two volunteers went down to the basement. They each had a torch, but as there was no electric light, the brightness of the torch beam only exaggerated the depth of the shadows. Gripping onto each other for moral support they called out the boy's name, again and again, but there was no response. Then, just when they were about to open the door to one of the storerooms at the back of the kitchen, they heard knocking from within. They opened the door, but instead of the shivering, nervous wreck they expected to see, in front of them was a cheerful boy who appeared well, although he wouldn't say anything. He was extremely cold, but overall he gave every appearance of being completely unharmed by his experiences. The one curious thing was that he seemed to be draped in an assorted jumble of scarves, jerseys, cardigans and gloves.

Anyway, since there was no way of getting him to answer any questions, Nick drove him back to the children's home. He and everyone else at The Regency Town House were grateful that the boy had been found unharmed. A few hours later there was a telephone call. It was the children's home to say that the boy who had been returned to them did not appear to be the same child as the one who had gone missing. All Nick could tell them was that, this time, there was no one left in the basement.

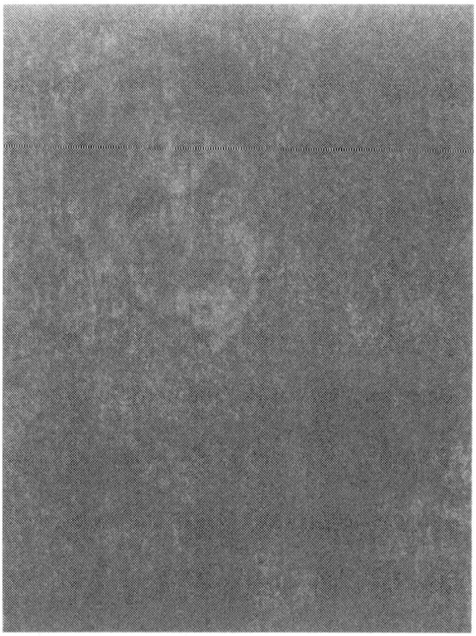

Table Manners

Ever since 1830, Thomson Hankey had sailed back to England from his plantations in Grenada and St Kitts, collected his wife and daughter from sleepy Tunbridge Wells and brought them to partake in society in Brighton for the summer season. The gaiety had obviously pleased him as in the early 1840s he wrote telling his wife that he planned to retire. He instructed her to lease a suitable house by the sea, furnish it and engage servants. Owing to Europe's almost insatiable desire for sugar, not only had he made a considerable profit, he had also been generously compensated for his slaves by the British government. He had finally decided to enjoy his profits as befits a gentleman. He did, however, caution his wife that on no account was she to purchase a dining table as he would be shipping home a glorious example made from beautiful tropical hardwood. The table apparently held memories of the good times he had enjoyed in the tropics.

Now released from an enforced sojourn in the country, Mrs Hankey applied herself with mounting enthusiasm to the task of finding suitable lodgings for her family. Brunswick Square was becoming very fashionable. Its clean air and relative proximity to London gave it great appeal for the winter season, particularly among parliamentarians, the nobility and their ladies. It seemed perfect for the Hankeys, and during the autumn of 1842 the female members of the household and a considerable staff moved into Number Ten.

They quickly set to work to redecorate in the latest style, furnish it and make it ready for the homecoming of its master. Amidst all this bustle, the arrival of a carter from Portsmouth, with the table from the Caribbean, passed almost without note. Martha, who at 28 was even more delighted than her mother at the move and her father's prospective return, was nevertheless feeling slightly superfluous to requirements. She decided that she alone would be responsible for the table's care once it had been assembled.

With a considerable amount of difficulty, it was taken into the empty dining room and fitted together. It was a very large table which could seat up to eighteen when fully extended. However, upon examination she could see that it had suffered considerably on the journey. The patina of the wood was dulled and, even after dusting, it failed to yield the lustre and sparkle about which her father had hinted. She resolved to undertake the task of bringing it back to its former glory and thus properly endear herself to her occasional parent whose arrival was much anticipated. She shooed the servant out of the room, donned an apron, then gathered some cloths and polish and began to work.

The table was so long she resolved to start at one end and make her way towards the other. She worked everyday. Indeed, she was soon doing very little else for she found it a most rewarding task. Gradually, as she polished, the table began to regain its brilliance. She understood why her father was so enamoured of it and reported excitedly to her mother that it was almost as though it was alive. When the evenings started to draw in and the room was lit by candles, the wood reflected their glow and to her great satisfaction she could see herself in the table's glistening surface. Enthusiastically she moved on towards the centre, but no matter how hard she polished, the wood in this section refused to release its brilliance. When she felt the surface, she detected that something had been dropped on it, candle wax perhaps, and despite all her efforts, the central leaves remained stubbornly dull. In frustration she decided to polish the other end, resolving to return to the centre later.

In a relatively short time, both ends of the table gleamed, shimmered, and reflected the light, as if the wood itself was dancing. But she knew that she had to go back and tackle its dark heart. To begin with she removed the wax cautiously with soft cloths being careful not to scratch the surface. Although she toiled day after day with polishing rags, she saw no improvement. It simply would not shine for her. What had once been a pleasure became almost a punishment, but Martha was a stubborn young woman and vowed not to be beaten. She stood at the task, she sat at the task, she cried, she railed at the table as though it could respond, but the central leaf remained dull and obscure. By this time, a winter chill had arrived and she felt the cold in the dining room most bitterly. The table became her obsession. She felt that it was almost holding out against her personally, that there must be secrets in the wood which it was refusing to divulge. She was determined that it should.

One late afternoon when she let herself in to the dining room, Martha immediately sensed that something had changed. The atmosphere seemed to envelop her. As she closed the door behind her, she became aware of the silence. All the ambient noise of the house and the street outside disappeared as though it had been sucked out and she was now in a vacuum. She found it hard to breathe. She walked to the table and looked down at the patch she had been rubbing. The wood had changed. It was gleaming now and it seemed to be moving and swirling so much that it almost made her feel giddy. Whereas the end sections of the table had seemed alive, glistening in response to any light shone upon them, this middle portion did not gleam or reflect her image, instead it appeared to be revealing movement and as she gazed upon it, shapes began to emerge.

Martha looked around realising that the change in the atmosphere of the room was because of the table. It wasn't just that she couldn't hear anything at all, she couldn't see clearly. There was some sort of haze in the room. Where she had been able to look out of the windows she could no longer make out where they were. There was even a faint smell of dead vegetation, overripe fruit and stagnant water. Now, instead of feeling excited and proprietorial towards the table, she was repelled by it and dreaded what she might see.

Nevertheless, she forced herself to look down at the centre once more. Slowly she began to discern figures in the wood and the face and outline of a woman carrying a candle and a cloth. Behind her there appeared the leering, overblown visage of a drunken man. He loomed nearer, grimacing with pleasure. The woman fell forward, her face distorted in agony and revulsion. The candle wax dripped.

Martha reeled away, ears ringing in the silence, eyes stinging in the foul mist as she gasped for air. She had immediately recognised the face of the man. It was her father.

With a strength of will she didn't know she had, she pulled the table at either end to release the leaves in order to stow them underneath. Then she pushed the ends together. In this manner the dreadful secret could be hidden. If ever there was to be a banquet in the house Martha knew that the table must always be covered since she now realised that nothing could eradicate the sin of her father, and it would be forever contained within the wood.

There is just a small postscript to this tale: When the Hankeys eventually moved from Number 10, there is a record from a renowned auction house that a very rare and valuable dining table achieved a great price. It could be anywhere now.

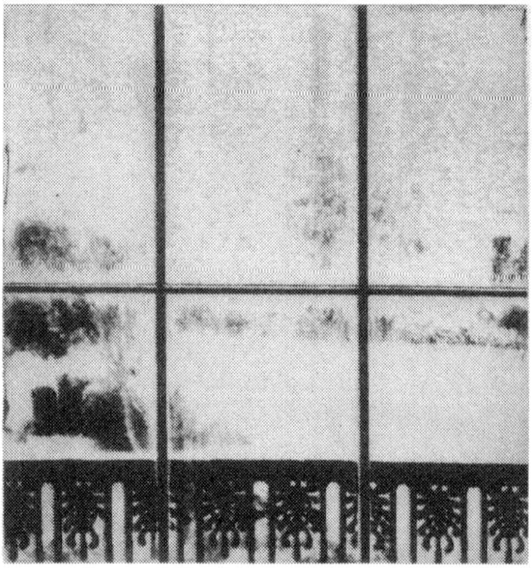

Through The Glass Darkly

November 5th had been a trial for Sadie ever since she was a small girl. It wasn't just the shock of a banger exploding at her feet that made her so afraid. It was also the implied danger and randomness of fireworks, the noise and the smell, and the simulated burning of a human being. She hated it. She felt the danger viscerally and when Mutt the terrier came to live with her, of course he felt just the same.

It was then that she recognised she was being

childish in sheltering under a duvet every year, so she began to seek other ways in which she and the dog could hide. That particular year she decided to retreat into the safety of the Regency Town House, where she was a volunteer, and do something useful as well as avoiding the festivities. The council had assured her that no bonfire night celebration was scheduled for Brunswick Square. Her rationale was that undisturbed, she could clear up the drawing room and then she and Mutt could sleep in the office until it was all over.

Before all light had finally left the sky, they both walked down the square. The day had been dark and looming. In fact, it had been one of those days which she thought was wrongly named. To her way of thinking it should be called an inter-night. The gusts of wind blowing up from the sea whipped the trees and scattered the leaves. The street lights suddenly went on, ironically adding menace to the strange shapes made by the tortured branches. Then, just as suddenly, they went off and the whole square was plunged into darkness. It didn't seem to matter, Mutt was happy and so was she because they were going to be all right once they were in the house.

She let herself in and flicked an unresponsive light switch. There obviously was a power cut, confirmed by a quick glance from the ground floor window. At least there were candles in the house and here she felt safe and invisible to the outside world and all its threats, real or imagined.

Just that day she had put new batteries in her torch in preparation for her nocturnal activities. So, armed with torch, ladder and black bin liners and followed faithfully by her hound, she marched into the drawing room on the first floor, determined to make a start on the clearing up. However, without any light from the outside, she was taken aback by quite how dark it was. She could see through the wild trees that the sea road was still lit as was the main road in the other direction. So it was just Brunswick Square which was affected. Never mind, she and Mutt would be fine in this house. She lit the stubs of candles around the room, turned off her torch, climbed the ladder and started unpinning the wilting foliage decorating the walls.

She worked steadily for some time, fully absorbed in her task. It was only when she had finished that she noticed that Mutt was whining. The pitiful little noise was unlike anything she had heard him make before. He sounded frightened, even terrified. She wanted to reassure him and followed the sound into the black corners and hidden recesses of the room. She found him cowering at the far end, half covered by a branch she had dropped. He would not move and continued to whimper. She looked around in the gloom for something that might lure him out. It was only then that she noticed the candles. Except for the one she was holding, they had all burnt out, but there was still light coming from outside. It couldn't be electricity because she had tried the switch again, but her curiosity drove her to look for the source of the light. Worried now, she could feel her skin beginning to crawl. She picked up the reluctant dog and went to the window.

What she saw made her gasp and step back, clutching Mutt closer to her. A shiver passed through both of them. Suddenly she was aware of the intense, loud, rapid beat of her heart and a ringing in her ears.

Gas street lights flickered brightly all over the square. On top of a bonfire sat a guy. The flames hadn't yet reached him, but they were beginning to lick hungrily from below. Hadn't the council said there would be nothing? But then she realised that the square itself was completely changed. There were no flower beds, no trees, no iron railings, no cars, no skip, and no tarmac. Nothing familiar to her. There was a dirt track where there should have been a road. She noticed two abandoned carts. In the middle of the square were planks of wood and piles of iron girders, stacks of bricks and mounds of flint and a lot of churned up mud. All of this was completely alien to Sadie, but it was there in front of her eyes, undeniable. She was mesmerised and utterly rooted to the spot. Perhaps she was just too tired and imagining it all, perhaps she was having a nightmare. But if so, it was one from which she couldn't wake up.

It was then that a group of people began to arrive. At first they came in dribs and drabs, gathering round the bonfire, warming their hands. The men were wearing breeches and long coats, the women were in long dresses with shawls and there were children too, some with nothing on their feet. As more and more spectators arrived, the scene in front of Sadie changed. The crowd was getting bigger and as it grew, people jostled each other, gently at first, but when a child threw a firework that landed at a man's feet he jumped and bumped into other people, who pushed him back. A Catherine Wheel was set alight and began to whizz round, faster and faster. Someone set off a rocket.

Nausea rising inside her, Sadie wanted to

scream at the chaos that she saw before her, but she couldn't utter a sound. Nothing she was seeing on the other side of the window was as it should be.

She could feel cold beads of sweat pricking her scalp and dribbling down her back. Mutt was trembling all the time. With a great effort she reasoned that they would be fine if they could not be seen, but it turned out that she and Mutt were just as visible to the people outside as they were to her. Some turned and began to point at her window. They conferred with each other and seemed as mystified as she was, but there were more of them, Sadie thought and she was alone.

They were an unruly, excitable crowd and now everybody was turning, pointing and looking at her. They abandoned their bonfire and began to walk towards the house. As they advanced Sadie panicked. The front door wouldn't withstand the weight of so many people and where a few moments ago she was just a spectator, she now felt vulnerable. If they were phantoms from the past, she wondered, what was she to them? Had she travelled back into their time and were they now seeing a glimpse of the future? She has become part of their story and she wasn't meant to be. Something fundamental that in the normal course of events keeps us going forward had been broken.

Suddenly she had an inspiration. She dropped Mutt and fumbled inside her coat for her torch which she shone directly at the crowd now gathering beneath the window. A very bright halogen light, a 21st century light that the crowd had never seen before, was beaming down at them. Gradually, they began to disperse. She kept the torch on until the first light of dawn when exhausted she fell asleep where she was on the floor.

When she woke up it was mid-morning and Mutt was beside her. The square was restored to its familiar self. At first she thought that the whole episode had been a nightmare. However the burnt circle of grass in the square suggested otherwise.

WITHIN THOSE WALLS

Until it happened, everyone thought very highly of Philip and his work. I didn't know him well - we were acquaintances rather than friends - but I was aware of his reputation. Having built an impeccable record as a forensic photographer he was much in demand. He was meticulous and at the same time very quick to get the results back to those who needed them. He was used not just by the police, but by archaeologists, historians and increasingly by conservationists.

When he worked for the police, he took pictures digitally because of speed, but for private commissions he much preferred to work with film. For him, the image that film recorded was the only reality that mattered and the detail, the graininess of celluloid and the chiaroscuro it offered, was in his opinion, unmatchable and he was gradually beginning to acquire a reputation not just as a photographer, but as an artist. But that night changed everything for him. What he told me has remained to haunt me in turn, so now I'm going to tell you.

While restoring a house in Brunswick Square, builders had found a box on the uppermost floor concealed in a wall behind the lathe and plaster. The conservationist was anxious to have it thoroughly recorded and photographed and then to put it back in the wall as soon as possible. Philip had been called in and given one night on which to capture images of the box and its contents.

After a busy day, he didn't get to the square

until the evening when the light was beginning to fade. Tired as he was, he still glanced up at the magnificent terrace of houses facing him through the trees. These houses, built in the 1820s, never failed to fill him with awe, but that evening he stopped in his tracks. He thought he could just make out a very faint white light coming from the windows on the upper two floors of the house to which he was going. He was sure that the builders had said there would be no one else there to disturb him, so he was mildly irritated. Maybe, he reasoned, someone had just left a light on by mistake.

All was quiet and still and dark when he let himself in. He lent back against the front door and called out, but he was answered with silence so he began to climb. As he trudged doggedly up the stairs with his heavy camera bag, the only sounds were the creaking floor boards under his feet. Once on the second floor landing, he peered through the open door to the bedroom beyond.

He was half expecting what he saw, but all the same it concerned him. This appeared to be the same white light that he had seen from outside and it was coming through the ceiling which had been stripped but not yet plastered. There was no electric light in the room, but there was definitely a radiance of some sort from a source that he couldn't make out. Now distinctly unsettled, he continued up the stairs to what had been the servants' quarters.

When he got there it was obvious that the source of the light he'd seen from outside and the floor below was on the other side of the door in front of him. Bracing himself for what he might find, he tentatively opened it. But he could see nothing. Wherever the source of the light, it was not, at least at that moment, in the room, which was completely dark. He quickly switched on the only working bulb that the builders had left him and at first glance there seemed nothing at all out of the ordinary. He could only see a small box, lying by itself on a white sheet in the middle of the floor.

He hadn't realised he was holding his breath until then, but now he let it out. He walked around the box and everything seemed perfectly in order. The builders had said it weighed almost nothing and it seemed very simple. It was made of unadorned pine and measured about 2 ft by 1 and, because it had lain undisturbed in the attic wall of the house since it had been built, the wood looked remarkably fresh and unmarked. He bent down to examine it more closely.

Immediately he reeled back. At close quarters it gave off a pungent, metallic odour. He gagged and his heart began to pound, but perhaps because of his tiredness, he didn't trust his own reactions. This, he reasoned, could all be imagined and he had to remind himself that his business was very much with the real.

He thought the best thing to do was just to get on with the job of photographing the box as quickly as possible and then go home.

He worked swiftly and assembled the special light he had brought with him. He liked the symbolism of a bright box on a sheet in the foreground surrounded by total blackness. The starkness of the image fitted the subject. This box had been alone in a wall for two hundred years. He started to take pictures. At first all went well as he moved around it and shot from every angle. He checked that the images were clear and the wood showed up well. Then the time came to photograph the interior as instructed, and he decided to prise the lid open using a chisel that he found in the decorator's tool kit.

As far as he knew, he was the first person to open the box since it had been placed in the wall and initially he approached the task with reverence, but to his dismay he found that he couldn't remove the lid. Having loosened the nails on one side, he moved over to the other only to find that the nails on the first side had somehow slipped back in to their holes as firmly as they had ever been. It felt as though the box was resisting him, as though it didn't want to be opened.

In the tool kit he found paint scrapers and this time when he loosened a nail he wedged one between the lid and the sides of the box. Eventually, with what seemed an enormous amount of wrenching out of all proportion to the size of the nails, he was finally able to prise the top from the box. It came away so suddenly that he fell backwards against his camera light, which immediately crashed to the floor and went out.

Surrounded by broken glass in the pitch dark, Philip felt afraid to his own surprise. He detected a more intense metallic smell and then, out of the gloom, he saw again the white light that he had observed from outside becoming clearer and clearer. It was coming from the box. Until that moment he had been able to rationalise his fears, but he knew now that he wasn't imagining this at all. He was completely alone with a malevolent force. He felt trapped, his heart was thumping so much he thought it might jump out of his chest and he sensed that he might somehow be nearing the edge of his reason.

However, Philip had always been a rational man at heart and, once again, he felt compelled to dismiss his fears and inch forward. On going closer, he could see a tiny stain of some sort on the white sheet. He was sure it had been unmarked when he'd first come into the room. As he stared the stain began to spread. Where there had been nothing, there was now definitely a blotch. Little by little it grew, and he saw too that the wood of the box, which had been so fresh and so smooth, was beginning to glisten with strange marks that showed up in the white light as if it was being attacked by an invisible claw. Whatever was happening to that box was happening now. He became aware of the silence surrounding him. In this almost tangible quiet, he heard a faint but terrible wail. It sounded like the wail of a baby.

Philip froze. His skin crawled and almost painfully each individual hair felt as though it was standing on end. Reluctantly and against every instinct, he forced himself to peer inside the box. As he lent over it, he thought he could make out a shape. Immediately, and without any hesitation this time, he knew that he had to get out of there, that by opening the box he had released something malign. Something terrible had happened here, in this room, and what was more it seemed to be happening again. With his camera flapping round his neck, he fled down the stairs, the noise of his departure muffling everything else.

A few days later he received a message from the conservationist asking that he return the key and saying that the builders had put the box back in the wall, had continued to plaster and paint and were nearly finished. She said they had cleared up the remains of his light, but made no mention of the box being open or of any marks on the surface of the wood, nor any stains on the sheet. On questioning her more closely, she didn't mention that they had found anything out of the ordinary at all.

Naturally she wanted to see the pictures he had taken. He had been reluctant to look before but now he went to find them. However, where there should have been pictures, there were just blank frames. He had no record whatsoever of that night except one: a close up of his own horrified face looking down, illuminated by a white light. He could just make out what might have been a dark undefined shadow behind him.

Philip burnt the camera film, but that night was effectively the end of his career. He was to discover that, because no one really believed his story, people gradually began to distance themselves. He lost work, drank too much and eventually could take the pressure no longer.

There is a buried secret, and I am haunted

by it. The malign force is contained...for now. I only wish I could remember the number of the house.

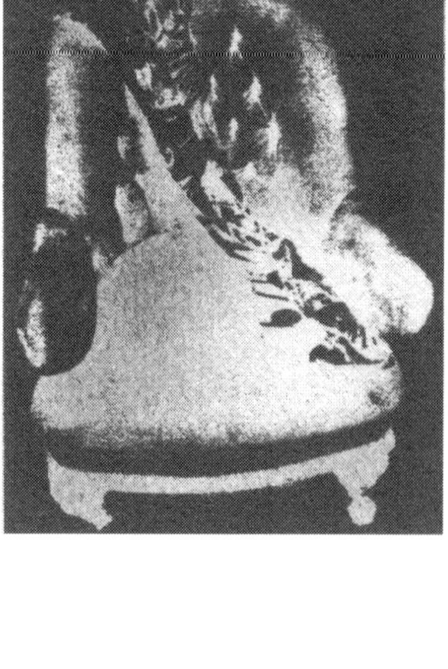

The Unlocked Room

She couldn't remotely afford to buy any of the tables, chairs, clocks, sofas, couches and ornaments from the 19th century that she handled every day in the auction room, though she coveted some of them desperately. She loved what people so dismissively called 'brown furniture'. The feel of dark polished wood made her wonder who had eaten at that table? Who had sat on those upholstered chairs? What had they talked about? And then there were those spectacular long case clocks. What had inspired their ornate decoration? Who had wound them and in what grand houses? And then there were the none-too-subtle sumptuous love seats. What had the people who once sat on them whispered to each other? Were they merely flirting?

Her days were spent in the heat of a lively imagination and the private fury of resentment at not being able to have any of this for herself. She was convinced that all this treasure was wasted on those whose only claim was that they could afford to buy. This was why she appreciated coming to The Regency Town House in Brunswick Square. She could spend time in a beautiful old house and yet there was nothing here to tempt her. There was no furniture to speak of and everything was rather shabby. It was a calm oasis which was full of students and volunteers during the daytime when she was never there, and always empty in the evenings when she was.

On the half landing on the way up to the office, she was used to passing the door of what she had been told was a small, empty room. She had never been in it, but on a particular evening in the autumn, on a whim she tried the handle. She was expecting resistance, but to her surprise it turned and the door creaked open. She paused, wondering what she might find on the other side, but felt compelled to push it open.

The light switch didn't work but she could just make out that this was a much deeper and longer room than she had anticipated. At first glance, there seemed to be nothing in it. Disappointed, she started to close the door, but as her eyes acclimatised she thought she saw something move. Tentatively, she opened the door wide again. This time her gaze was directed straight to a little Victorian button-back chair in the far corner by a window. How had she missed it? From where she stood it appeared to be covered in a dark material and she was struck by its elegance and beauty. It looked perfect.

She drew in her breath. She couldn't resist. She was drawn to it, but when she neared the chair she shivered involuntarily. The air in that part of the room was fractionally colder. She sensed a draught and was looking around in the gloom for its source when suddenly the door slammed shut. The noise startled her and the room was plunged into complete darkness.

She stood quite still and gradually she was able to make out the beautiful chair, which appeared to be lit by a shaft of moonlight coming through the window. It was covered with a lush red velvet and when she put her hand out to touch, it felt soft, slightly warm, luxurious and very inviting. Breathing hard with anticipation, she lowered herself into the chair and immediately felt deliciously comfortable as she leant back into its embrace. Had she not known better, she might have thought that the chair was settling itself around her, protecting her from the cold. She gave herself up to the pleasure of imagining herself surrounded by adoring children. She was going to tell them a pre-bedtime story and their upturned expectant faces radiated happiness and contentment. She leant back and closed her eyes.

Then she felt something. Her eyes snapped open. Her fantasy left as suddenly as it had come, her body was rigid and she held her breath. Tentatively she moved her hand to properly investigate what it was that had touched her. It was just a scarf on the arm of the chair, a very beautiful scarf with deep purples that swirled in random patterns. Perhaps it had been camouflaged, but it was still strange that she hadn't noticed it before. How could she keep missing things? It was so unlike her.

Distracted, she picked it up and draped it around herself and leaned back even further into the chair. After a while she managed to lose herself once again this time in imagining what it would have been like to be a daughter of the house and to have sat here when everything was new and adventure was before her. She was lost in yet another fantasy when she felt the scarf tighten slightly around her neck.

She loosened it. She must have sat on the end

of it she decided and sank back into the chair once more. The same thing happened again, only this time she felt a distinct jerk as though it was being pulled. Frightened now, she felt she had to make sure that there was no one else there, no one tugging it. Rationally of course, she knew she was alone, but she still turned her head and looked behind her just to be certain.

Again she thought she caught a movement out of the corner of her eye. The window was open. That would account for the chill and the draught, she thought, although she was sure it was closed when she had first come into the room. It was then she began to smell something fetid, unpleasant. Maybe it was coming from outside.

The answer to all this was simple, of course, she needed to close the window, but when she tried to get up to do so she couldn't move. She even had trouble leaning forward. The chair didn't want to let her go. It was ridiculous, but there was no denying that she couldn't get up. She was trapped. Meanwhile the cold and the smell were getting stronger.

It was then that she became aware of the silence. She couldn't hear anything at all through the open window: no sea gulls calling, no radios, no noise from nearby kitchens. How long had this intense silence been going on for? How long had this strange separation from the outside world been enveloping this little room? Here inside, the sound was muffled as though she was hearing things from beneath a blanket or in snow. She tapped her feet, but she heard absolutely nothing. The silence had cut her off from the real world.

Forced to sit back, she felt the scarf tightening one more notch around her neck. It was becoming difficult to breath. She was in danger of choking. What had seemed an invitation to sit down she now saw as a self-indulgence of her own making. If she hadn't given way to her imaginings, she wouldn't be trapped in this chair. The fantasy she had conjured up was turning very sour. It had become reality, and it was threatening her. This chair and this scarf were weaving her into their history. And something was very wrong in that history.

By now truly frightened, she panicked. She grasped the tightening scarf and with a supreme effort pulled it as free of her neck as far as she could. At the same time she kicked out violently, swearing and screaming at the very top of her voice. She knew that she had to break through that wall of silence. With every fibre of her being, she tried to free herself from chair and further loosen the scarf. Nothing happened. The chair imprisoned her: the scarf was still tight around her neck. But she didn't stop screaming, she shouted, she used language that she didn't even know she knew, she moved every sinew of her body in order to free herself, she fought. The window was open, surely someone must hear her.

And finally the raucous noises she was making broke the silence and the malign spell was shattered. She felt the scarf loosening and she leapt from the chair, ran from the room, down the stairs and out of the house.

She phoned the Regency Town House the next day to say she wouldn't be returning but as she tried to explain why, she was met with disbelief.

"There's nothing in that room," she was told. "The door's locked and we lost the key some time ago."

The mark around her neck told a different story.

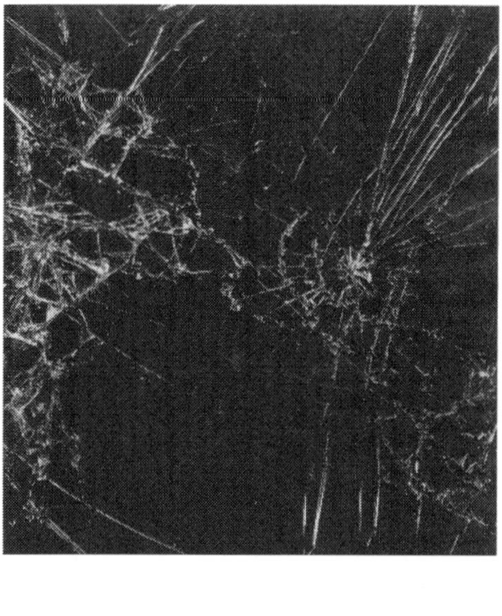

The Anthaeum (A Nearly True Story)

Finally, James thought, a job that suited him. He would create his own world. As an experienced gardener, he had been appointed to tidy up Palmeira Square after the summer, to plant it out and to enable it, in the words of the local government lackey who had hired him, "to return to its former glory". He had no idea what its former glory was, but he could see that now it was a mess and there would have to be a lot of weeding, digging and cutting before he could decide what to do with it. He knelt on the soft grass beside the top bed and started forking the soil. He was working diligently and was pleased with the progress he was making when his fork hit something hard.

He reached out with his hands. Gently scraping the earth away, he revealed a corner of an object which resisted when he pulled. Whatever it was seemed deeply buried. The top was angular and sharp and covered in dirt, but a tell-tale glint suggested that it was a piece of glass. He couldn't leave it where it was, so he started to loosen the earth and carefully made a channel around it.

Gradually, very gradually, as James dug down he could see that he was uncovering a rectangle of glass that looked thinner and more fragile than a pane in any window he had ever seen. Strange he thought, that it hadn't already broken. It took him a good two hours to almost free it, but sitting on his haunches he tugged and was able to loosen the whole piece. It was big and unwieldy and when it did come out, there was a sudden whoosh almost as though it was happy to be liberated. He rolled over on his back, but he was holding it and it was still intact.

Carrying it very carefully, he took it over to the standpipe and washed off the earth. He felt weary and sat down on the nearest bench to look at his discovery, now propped up against his bag. It was getting towards evening and the sun caught the glass which reflected the light back at him. It was too bright and it almost blinded him so he moved along the bench to get out of the glare, but he found that he couldn't escape from it. The magnified, fierce rays seemed to be trapping him, wherever he went. He was very tired after his work and this wasn't helping, so he closed his eyes for a moment. He didn't know how long his eyes were shut, but when he opened them nothing that he was expecting to see was there.

Palmeira Square itself seemed to have disappeared and where there should have been houses, buses, cars and in the distance, a road, there were only fields. Everything the least bit familiar had gone. He was still sitting on a bench but now it was dwarfed inside an enormous dome made entirely of iron arches and glass panels which rose to a central cupola. He closed his eyes again, not believing them and thinking maybe the effort of freeing the glass had taken more out of him than he'd realised at the time. But when he opened them again, he was still in this glittering cathedral. The whole seemed to be supported by a wooden column, but that hardly detracted from the gigantic conservatory. The piece of glass he had laboured to release from the earth looked as though it was the same size as the ones in the dome.

James was too amazed to be properly frightened. He gazed around in wonder and where he normally avoided people, on this occasion he determined to find someone to ask what on earth was going on. He stood up, and it was only then that he saw what the magnificent dome housed.

Sheltering under it, and thus out of the blustery inclement weather outside, he found himself in another world. A few feet from where he stood, a small lake with a carpet of luxurious white waterlilies faded into the distance. A family of ducks were swimming in formation, tree swallows were drinking on the wing and cheeping sparrows were flitting from branch to branch of native and tropical trees, which were planted at irregular intervals. James could see a seagull on the other side of the glass dome, struggling against the wind to maintain its position, but the birds inside were unaffected by the gusts outside. Gravel paths ran beside the lake, with benches at regular intervals beside them. The paths wandered all over the place and even lead up into a small copse on a hill. In between the paths and the trees, plants of all kinds were thriving, some flowers were blooming out of season and yet more potted plants were scattered here and there ready to go into the soil. All this colour and life was being nurtured and protected under the magical rotunda.

However, there was nobody there and he walked up one of the paths towards the cupola in the centre of the dome. He had only gone a few feet when he heard voices. They seemed to be raised, to be shouting, even screaming. He hurried towards the sound, but stopped suddenly when he saw four men in the distance. Two were wearing top hats, spats, fitted coats, neckties and were waving their walking sticks at one who was dressed similarly but lacked a hat. Another man stood to one side with a dejected air saying nothing. They came from another era and it was then that James realised he, himself, was wearing rough, brown leather boots and thick socks, a linen smock and corduroy breeches. Evidently he was still a gardener, but not dressed as any gardener he recognized. The entire scene was so strange and unworldly that he had great difficulty believing any of it, and yet his hand still ached from all the digging he'd done, and in his heart he knew it was real enough.

As he got nearer to the men who were arguing he could make out some of what they were saying.

"For God's sake man, it will fall down, you

must see that," shouted one of the top hatted men, who James reckoned to be one of the bosses.

"Mr Wilds is right. I am an engineer, I designed this place and I know it cannot hold," said the other, "I want nothing more to do with this hare-brained project. You may be the contractor English, but I know what I'm talking about." With that he turned on his heels and strode away into the distance, shortly followed by his companion.

"You lily-livered ninnies. I'll show you. I'll show you. You've never dirtied your hands in your lives. I have, I know what I'm talking about." James saw that the man called English was trembling with anger.

The sad figure who had been standing to one side and who James had hardly noticed, turned to him and said, "Please, English, before you do anything let me consult another engineer."

"Go, away Mr Phillips, leave it to me. All will be well, you'll see." And with that he ran up into the copse and disappeared on the other side of the hill, leaving a dejected Mr Phillips to follow in the wake of the other two, now distant, figures.

James was just about to follow when the fellow called English re-emerged this time accompanied by six burly men.

"Take that down," he instructed, gesturing at the wooden column in the middle of the dome. "I'll show them. They think they know best, but it's me who's done the work, and it's me who knows what's what around here". With that the six men set to: they wheeled a scaffold tower into position, climbed it and started to dismantle, plank by plank, the support column. James watched with horror, now understanding only too well the reason for the row he had overheard.

He decided in a flash that discretion was the better part of valour, so he crouched down near a flower bed pretending to do some planting, while watching what was going on. Soon the men had dismantled the column. The dome held up despite the force of the wind on the outside. English was triumphant. He crowed ceaselessly and finally, after clapping everyone on the back, he sent the men home. Having taken one last inspection, he made a sweeping bow to the cupola and strode off, shouting over his shoulder, "Lock up my man. See you tomorrow."

James was reluctant to leave and found himself not only planting the pot in his hand, but soon reaching for another one. He began to fantasise. Perhaps he could stay here. This, after all, was definitely the garden's former glory.

It was late August and the sun was setting. As the light leached from the sky outside so did the colour leach from the glasshouse. Plants closed their flowers and where once the lake sparkled, the water in it now began to look black. The bird song that was so loud and cheerful half an hour ago, now quieted until it hushed altogether. The silence inside the dome made the whine of the wind outside more threatening. James could see trees bending and shaking as the gusts became stronger. To his horror, he saw the dome itself was slowly swaying. Suddenly he heard a report like the running fire of light artillery. The glass was breaking. An immense galaxy of sparks produced a powerful flash of light. The iron girders were bending. Dropping his tools, he ran for his life.

Postscript:

The Anthaeum was the brainchild of Henry Phillips, a local botanist, horticulturalist and landscape gardener. He had already worked with the architect A.H. Wilds on the laying out of the Level in 1822 and on the layout of the Kemptown Enclosures. He had published books and drawn up plans for parks and gardens all over Brighton. The Anthaeum was originally a scheme for what he called Oriental Gardens, which were to be part of the development of Oriental Place. That never happened but his plans were revived for a site north of Adelaide Crescent. The enormous dome covered an area of more than an acre and a half and was intended to be much as described in the story.

It was built between 1832 and 1833 and was visited by Joseph Paxton (who built the Great Conservatory at Chatsworth and the Crystal Palace), but when it was nearing completion, the contractor proposed abandoning the central supporting pillar. Wilds and Hollis, the engineer resigned and before Phillips could consult another engineer, the contractor removed the support on 29th August 1833. The Anthaeum collapsed with no fatalities, the head gardener having escaped with his life. Henry Phillips went blind from the shock and the twisted iron and glass remained where it had fallen for 20 years.

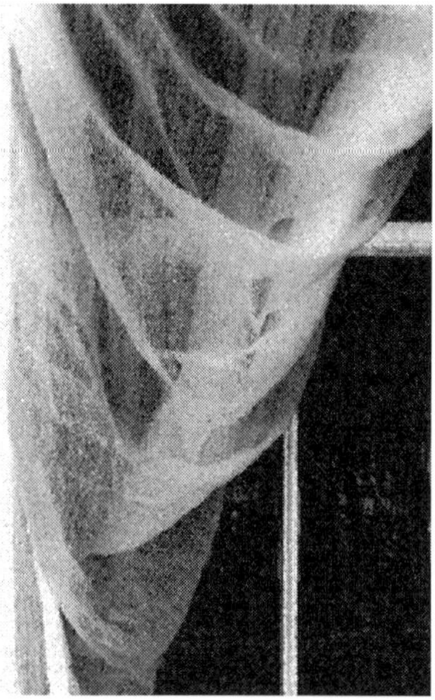

Screensaver

Full of hope, Gemma stepped jauntily down from the bus at the top of Brunswick Square and, as though in slow motion, immediately stumbled and fell on the thick blanket of slippery leaves. Her bag and papers scattered on the pavement as she held her hand out to break her fall. She would just have to pray that all her precious research, recorded so painstakingly on her computer, was still there. She was especially excited because from her discoveries that very day, she thought she might at last be on the path to clarity about the notorious events that had culminated in a suspicious death.

Since no one was around to help her up - or thankfully to witness her humiliation - she could unashamedly give way to self-pity. She painfully scrambled to her feet, registered the large hole in her tights, and nursing her sore ankle and wrist, collected her jumbled belongings and slowly started to hobble down the side of the square.

"Pride comes before a fall, quite literally," she mumbled out loud, her spirits, a minute ago so buoyant, now deflated. What she needed, she thought, was a glass of wine.

Because she was making such slow progress, she had time to take in her surroundings. A week before she had been lucky enough to be able to move in to the very flat where the research subject of her latest 'true crime' book had lived just 40 years before. In as much as it was possible, she had always wanted to have some of the same experiences as her subjects. It gave her an unique perspective and was something she stressed whenever she pitched to publishers who showed an interest in her work. Immersing herself in the atmosphere of a location, and then taking people's imaginations on a journey which had nothing to do with their daily circumstances, had reaped rewards in the past and she was even fantasising about a television series.

Until now she had not had time to look around, but that evening she saw that the street lights were barely adequate and that they showed the square in a monochrome twilight. She had always thought that these houses were the epitome of elegance, but in that dim light their blank, yellowish exteriors interspaced with empty, black windows, appeared threatening. In places they needed new plaster and paint, several of the rusty iron gates down to the basements were hanging off their hinges and the grass in the centre looked uncared for. In the period she was researching,the council had wanted to pull down the square because it was so dilapidated and in this gloom it didn't seem as though much had changed. This was a cold place.

Eventually Gemma arrived at her front door. Painfully she got out her key and, concentrating hard because she had jammed things into her bag after the fall and didn't want to spill them, she opened it. As soon as she did so, she felt a strong cold draught from the inside and staggered as somebody brushed past and tumbled down the steps in a great hurry. Gemma had had no time to move aside and it felt almost as though something had moved through her. She reeled against the door, shocked and feeling sick.

Her legs felt as though they would collaspe and she had to sit down there and then. As she did so she came to a realisation. There had been something familiar about the figure that had rushed past. She had seen that face before. Where? Who was it?

Gemma felt the wind had been knocked out

of her. Her heart was beating fast. She wanted to leave, to get out, to go somewhere else, but she had nowhere else to go so she got up slowly and climbed the stairs to her flat. She was aware of how alone she was. Once inside, she went to the window and was immediately struck by how impenetrably dark it seemed to have become. The evenning had gone from dusk to pitch black in the time it had taken her to climb the stairs and the houses on the other side of the square now looked even more threatening. She quickly closed the curtains and turned around to review the room.

Her Christmas cards and a few party invitations were in place on the mantelpiece above the fireplace, but as she stood with her back to the window, she noticed in the mirror that the curtains behind her were twitching just a little as though something was moving them.

When she turned again, the curtains were still. She knew that the window was closed but it felt as though she was being watched.

Logically she was certain that there was no one there, but she couldn't help but be uneasy. Maybe she had allowed herself to identify too personally with the story she was researching. Bringing dark histories to life, which was her speciality, definitely had its drawbacks. But the movement in the curtain had been real and, however much she rationalised her fear, she still felt as though she wasn't completely alone. Her thoughts kept returning to what had happened downstairs and that strange figure at the door.

She poured a glass of white wine and tried to reason with herself. Now, sitting in a comfortable chair, she glanced around. It was then that she started to notice the difference between the way she thought she had left things and the way they were now.

Her room looked dishevelled and messy. There was no water in the vase on the mantelpiece and the flowers were drooping for lack of it. Her favourite shoes were lying carelessly abandoned by the sofa and one had its heel broken in two. Her hairbrush was matted with hair and sitting in a pool of spilt coffee on the table. She had no memory at all of leaving things like this. She was sure she had put water in the vase, knew she would never have left the hairbrush sitting in coffee, and was convinced that she hadn't broken a heel. Someone had been in her flat. Someone had done this. She didn't dare inspect the hairbrush. She feared to find that the hair in it was not her own.

Chaos was laid out plainly in front of her eyes and seeing it so clearly had the effect of making her doubt herself. Was she really as neat and ordered as she liked to think? She even wondered if she might be going mad.

Gemma shivered violently. The radiators were hot, but that made no difference. She was expecting something to happen, but didn't know what and she couldn't bear the waiting. In her anxiety, she turned to the only immediately familiar place she could think of – she opened her computer intending to distract herself but now she realised where she'd seen the woman at the front door. That same face confronted her on her computer. Her research subject however, had died 40 years previously. The eyes on the screensaver seemed to be watching her. She slammed the laptop shut, she would get no comfort there.

Her pulse raced, but all the same she tried to analyse the events leading up to this evening. She had thought she had been fortunate to live in the same flat in which her subject had been found. Now, she was not sure that this had been a lucky coincidence at all. She panicked. She only had herself to blame...she had wanted to be immersed in atmosphere and now the atmosphere had trapped her. She slowly realised, it wasn't just atmosphere she had been immersed in, she had started to identify herself with the woman who had been accused of carrying out a very dark crime. She thought she had made some sort of breakthrough, and maybe she had, but perhaps it was a breakthrough in identity. Perhaps she was getting very close to understanding her subject...too close. Could this all be a warning of some kind?

Her fevered, chaotic thoughts were interrupted by a persistent scraping at the window. But there was no tree outside her window and no branches which could possibly be blown against it.

It sounded as if someone wanted to get in. She pulled a blanket around herself in denial and lay on the sofa half frozen, and very, very frightened. She dug her nails into her hands and waited but she didn't know what for. She wouldn't sleep, she at least knew that.

Dawn came and Gemma stumbled from the sofa and looked around. All the things that struck her as odd the night before were still there, but now, in the faint growing light, she saw that the wine glass she had drunk from was on the table beside her sodden hair brush. It had the remnants of a thick, dark red liquid inside it. She looked at the mantlepiece and froze. All her Christmas cards were upside down and some had fallen to the floor. Her invitations had been turned around so that all she could see was blank card, signifying nothing. Their very presence seemed to mock her. During the night her flat must bhvnight her flat must have been visited again, but she didn't know when or how and she felt that none of this belonged to her.

There seemed to be one clear message in all of this. What she was about to find out was too dark, too difficult, too personal, and she had got too near. If she wanted a quiet life she would have to abandon her research, and with it all her hopes for the future.

She opened her laptop and, not looking at the face staring out at her, deleted all her work from her computer and the Cloud. She sat back and breathed deeply.

Sometime later she turned her laptop on again. But it didn't go to the blank screen she had expected. The face that she had tried to erase stared out at her, triumphant. Too late she realised she might never be free.

All In The Family

Stripping firms of their assets had never posed her any moral quandaries and over the many years she had done it, she had invested in what some people would call deeply questionable ventures. Her sole justification had ben profit and she had chosen never to take into consideration the malign and personal effects of her actions which ranged from bankruptcies, to homelessness, to children taken into care, and even suicide on two occasions. She had always made sure to stay just on the right side of the law.

She was and always had been completely and wilfully blind to what other people, especially her family, held against her. She could admit that she was sometimes a bit dogmatic and easily lost her temper when people argued with her, since she had proved, year after year, that she was right. Over time she had made enough money for everyone to live well. Indeed they had lived very well thanks to her, yet they were all ungrateful. Now she was a very rich woman with beautifully coiffed hair, lacquered nails and despite her years, still cutting a perfect figure in designer clothes. She was well regarded in some rather dubious circles while managing to alienate everyone who had ever been close to her.

She told herself that this didn't matter a jot because she nursed a secret which provided her with all the love that she could not get from her family: her collection of priceless antiques.Safe in her eerie, they provided a calming refuge, a haven of peace and security. Every stick of furniture had a story and a personality, and they all belonged to her. Care and attention had gone into restoring the exquisite and valuable display in front of her. If people were so stupid that they could not bear to be in the same room with her, then their goods and chattels were the next best thing. She understood people, the trouble was that they did not understand themselves and thought that they did not need her. Well, she knew that they did.

What gave her particular peace was that furniture didn't answer back. Over the years these pieces, all once the prized possessions of various relatives, had become her true friends, her real family. Her own flesh and blood were now dead to her, but their possessions were reliable and she knew to the centimetre where everything should be. It was a great pleasure to rearrange them, to invent stories pretending that her relatives were as submissive as this furniture. She was always involved in these stories and they always turned out well, and in her favour. In her imagination everyone was always very grateful and pathetically apologetic for the way they had mis-judged her. Until now.

Something was wrong. She sensed it from the minute she entered the room that night, but all the same she felt compelled to follow her routine. So she did what she always did, she lit the fire and the candles, and then with her back to the fireplace and the mirror above it, surveyed the scene and tried to discern what could possibly have upset her.

Something was out of place. That was it. Her sharp eyes scanned the room and came back to rest on the silver topped cane. She was sure that it was not where she had left it. It was only a little thing, but it was by attending to the little things that she had made her fortune. Her heart beat faster. The cane lay across a chair when she could have sworn that she had propped it up by the clock. She shivered involuntarily. This had never happened before, but the fact remained that the top of the cane was glistening in the firelight and had she not known better, she would have thought someone had just put it down.

The cane was once particularly dear to her useless son, but the idiot boy had had no alternative but to give it to her in exchange for yet another settlement of his debts. That had been the final parting of the ways. The parasite had complained loudly to his siblings, and no one from the family had been in touch since. That was years ago, and for all she knew - or cared - her son had died of his addiction. However, this reminiscence was all quite ridiculous, she thought as she stepped forward to put the cane back in its rightful place.

She stopped short when she touched it. It felt clammy and very cold, almost as if it were resisting her. Nevertheless she moved it, then walked back to the fireplace.

What she saw in the mirror above the mantelpiece made her gasp. Her scalp prickled.

She dug her long nails into the palms of her hands, trying to keep a sense of reality. There must be something wrong with the reflection, she thought. The candles flickered as though there was a draught, but there was none. The room looked much darker than she knew it actually was, and the sides of the long case clock appeared to be moving. To begin with she thought she must be seeing things that weren't there and wiped her eyes with a corner of her blouse, but it made no difference. The clock's hands were pointing to five minutes to midnight when she knew that midnight had already chimed. She realised, with complete certainty, that for the first time in her adult life, she had no control and in this of all places, her own designated realm. Her stomach churned. She suddenly felt her aloneness almost viscerally.

She swung around to look at the room and in those few seconds it was returned to order. Then, for some inexplicable reason, she found herself compelled to turn back to the mirror and survey the reflection in it again.

What she saw now chilled her to the bone. It was the same room, but it seemed to be altering as she looked. The quivering candlelight appeared more intense and created deep shadows and dark corners where she knew there were none. The furniture was no longer neutral, no longer benign. Its position was slowly changing, as though it had a will of its own. There was freedom, independence where there had been none. Nothing was hers anymore.

The silence was cut by the clock which began to strike - slowly. She wanted to close her eyes and turn away from the mirror, but she found herself trapped by the image she saw there. The Victorian chair, once her mother's, was toppled over on its back; the drawers of a Dutch chest, once her cousin's, were flung across the room; a carving which had belonged to her nephew had slipped down the wall; her daughter's long case clock was thrown forward and an aunt's antique flat iron had smashed her niece's Meissen Porcelain dinner service. The only sound was that of the clock which chimed on and on relentlessly. If the rightful owners couldn't have the furniture, she certainly wasn't going to have it.

Then she saw that the walls were closing in. The space behind her was getting very slowly smaller. Her own terrified face looked back at her from the mirror, her eyes taking in the alien chaos. And it was then that she saw again, with horror, the cane with the silver top.

It was held in the fist of a man who was emerging from the shadows. At first she thought this was a stranger, but as he came closer he to looked familiar. The man took another step. Surrounded by the ever darker and more claustrophobic room, the looming figure raised the stick with its glittering silver top as if to strike. The attacker was her son.

With what little rational mind she had left, the old woman, for by now she had become her true age, realised that she had to turn around, she had to change.

Was it too late?

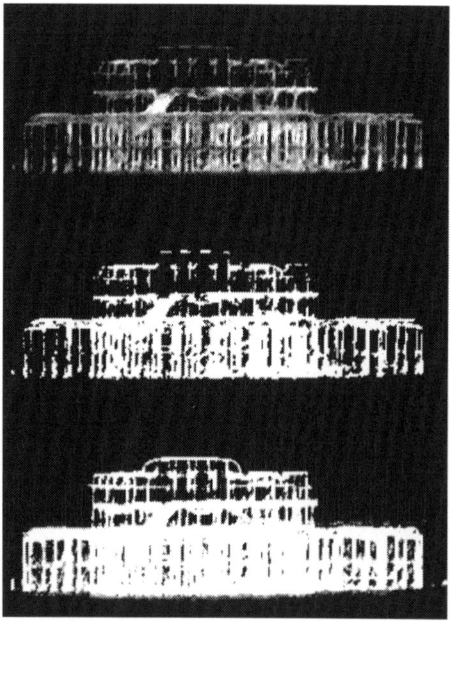

The Sea Fret

Suitably attired for the street, Reggie looked at himself in the mirror and by sheer force of habit twirled around, although he had to admit it was more of a shuffle these days. He might be in his ninth decade he thought, but he would always make sure that he cut a dashing figure. Albeit threadbare, his multi-coloured embroidered waistcoat peeped jauntily from beneath his corduroy blazer and he made a dapper figure when he smiled and tipped his hat at his neighbour on the steps outside. She could never have guessed that he was preoccupied by something that had been niggling at him, but which he couldn't quite identify. He had decided to clear his thoughts by doing what he used to do before his arthritis had become so painful, walk to Brighton and back.

As a veteran variety entertainer, he was steeped in the philosophy that the show must go on so, although his limp made the progress slow and somewhat painful, he never once thought of turning back. It was a dark, clear night and his feet resounded unevenly on the pavement as he limped down Brunswick Square. It was good to be out and when the familiar and relentless hum of traffic on Kingsway had paused long enough to let him cross, he hobbled the width of the lawns and turned left with determination.

What he hadn't bargained for was a sea fret that suddenly reared up in front of him. Resolved to understand whatever was troubling him, he decided to go on, so he walked into it and was immediately enveloped in a cloud so dense it blocked the streetlight, deadened sound, and rendered his familiar surroundings alien. Impenetrable walls confronted him and then as quickly as they had appeared, they disappeared. He was alarmed to find distances expanding and contracting as unfamiliar shapes loomed out of nowhere. The fog had become a shapeshifting monster.

He almost bumped into The Meeting Place café before he realised what it was. Now it was closed, barricaded against the weather. He hobbled on but once past the hut, the terrain became foreign. The fog seemed to be teasing him, playing with him, daring him to recognise somewhere, only for him to realise he couldn't recognise anywhere. The wall on the left stopped quite abruptly and now there was only the path. Very slowly he followed the curves beneath his feet, but he knew from memory that there was no structure on either side and he felt strangely unsupported. He wasn't exactly afraid, but the silence disturbed him so he decided to go down onto the shingle where at least he could hear the crunch beneath his feet as he trudged on.

After struggling painfully over the stones for a few metres he was forced to admit defeat. His knee was hurting badly so he sat down and tried to pinpoint what had brought him out in the first place. To his consternation his mind seemed as blank as his surroundings, yet he reasoned, something must have happened to make him feel so ill at ease. The sea fret suited his mood. He felt hopelessly lost in a world that was lost.

As he stared into the greyish-black cotton wool, he began to distinguish differences in the fog. It was constantly moving and changing, sometimes more dense and sometimes less. For an instant he caught a glimpse of an enormous free-standing column immediately in front of him, but in the very next instant the image was gone. That must surely be the West Pier, he thought. It was closer than he had realised. This had been his old stomping ground, although when passing it nowadays he avoided looking at it, for reasons he had never been able to fathom. In his present situation he had no choice, however, so with dread in his heart he sat and waited, wondering what it was that he had just seen.

The fog cleared again and this time he was able to take in more of the scene rearing high above him. The Pier was almost on top of him. But it wasn't as he knew it to be – a solitary skeleton of abandoned cast iron – instead it was whole, unscathed, intact, gleaming white and just as he had known it in the old days. Reggie began to feel sick with an unexplained and dreadful anticipation. He hadn't had this feeling for a long time, but it was somehow horribly familiar. He wanted to stop whatever was happening, but he had no idea how. He was forced to watch and as he did so, he began to pick out details. Everything seemed newly painted, there were lights strung along the promenade deck and at the entrance to the central amusement arcade and the concert hall pavilion at the far end. This was unreal, he reasoned. He was seeing things that weren't there but, despite telling himself that, nothing changed. The pier was perfectly solid. It looked pristine and inviting with a glass panel in the centre, which reflected the lights and the surrounding balustrade. However, the fog was constantly moving and as it swirled up again the image disappeared in front of his eyes.

Transfixed now, he kept staring at the same place. Before long, the resurrected pier showed itself again, but this time it had come to life with people walking towards the concert hall. From where he sat he glimpsed men wearing wide trousers with turn ups and girls swinging handbags, disporting full skirts and displaying lots of seamed stockinged leg. People were smoking and talking to each other excitedly, in groups, in couples, some with children and some without. He could hear a Dean Martin recording welcoming people. He could even catch snatches of conversation, all of it joyous.

"Looking forward to it."

"I've heard he's so funny."

"Alf told me he's definitely one to watch."

"Darling, you're going to love this."

A laughing couple pointed to the posters plastered all over the front of the concert hall. They displayed a photograph and a name in red letters which had a sticker plastered diagonally over it.

Somebody said, indicating the sticker, "Ridiculous! Don't know what that's about."

Somebody else agreed "Must be a mistake. I've heard him before and he's good."

Everyone was cheerful. They had come here for a good time. He could only watch as streams of happy people surged onwards. And then, after what seemed like an age, he saw the doors of the pavilion theatre close behind the crowd.

Quite suddenly it was silent. He imagined that inside everyone was full of anticipation, finding their seats, rustling their programmes, buzzing with excitement, but here, now, with the doors closed all was still and quiet.

Faint at first, and then gradually becoming more distinct, came the unmistakable sound of cat calling, slow hand clapping, stamping of feet, jeering and booing.

Sitting on the shingles, Reggie felt the urge to shout. He opened his mouth but what came out was a whimper that disappeared into the damp air. Slowly and with great difficulty, he managed to get to his feet and peer more closely at the poster. It only confirmed what he already knew. He recognised the unmistakable face. The name written underneath was his. The banner pasted over it said clearly "Final performance: Tour cancelled". Now he understood, now it was coming back to him.

A familiar figure emerged from the far end of the pavilion, glanced behind him and, apparently fearful that he would be caught, ran down the length of the pier. He caught a glimpse of his own young, terrified self.

The next moment the fog obliterated

everything and when it cleared again, the West Pier was once again the familiar abandoned wreck. Tears were rolling down Reggie's cheeks. Once more he had been present on the night he died.

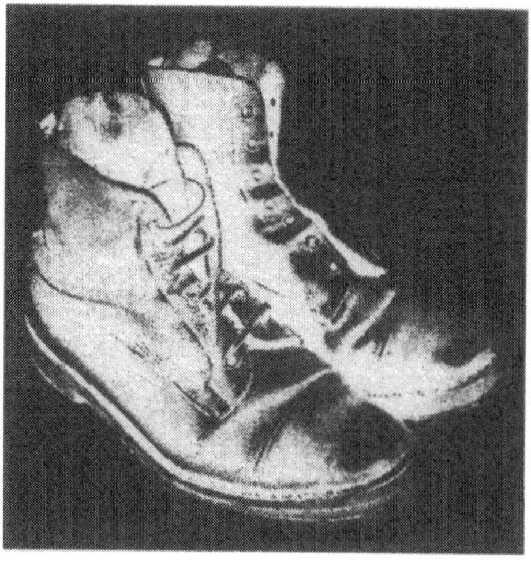

The Soldier's Return

Simon was alone as he limped up Brunswick Square, but he was used to that and it was how he preferred things now.

Back in Brighton in 1918, yet it seemed only yesterday to have been 1914 - how strange. He'd been just a boy when his mother had begun bringing him down on the train to pay awkward visits to his grandmother. He could hardly remember the old lady but, now he thought about it, he did remember that she had a particular smell. Yardley's Lavender Water. Those visits had stopped only five years ago, but it felt like another lifetime. Time had telescoped from both ends but evidently the old lady had died and left her tiny flat, and a very small inheritance, to him. How unreal it all was. How peculiar.

He could remember the excitement he had felt at seeing the sea for the first time. Now it was as though he was being told about his memories, as though it hadn't happened to him. He recognised it to be a kind of numbness, but he didn't care, in fact he welcomed it. It was better that way. He had learnt how to shut his emotions down, to put out their fire and he was content that that was how it was going to be. It meant he couldn't be hurt and so he wouldn't hurt others.

Badly wounded, he had been brought home by the Red Cross, after a short stay in a field hospital in the tunnels beneath Arras. He was grateful to his nearly shattered leg, because he knew it masked a much greater injury. Whereas some of his fellow patients screamed, ranted, threw things, wept; he had gradually withdrawn. He found that he could choose whether to recall events or not and that it was easier not to, because burying them was simpler. At first he felt guilty, as though by not remembering he was dishonouring his dead friends, but he discovered he was also able to put his guilt to one side. He could survive as long as he lived a very quiet, strict and ordered life on his own terms, which meant eschewing other people and avoiding crowds.

At last he reached the one tall imposing terraced house which he found vaguely familiar. In a sea of similar houses, this one was almost indistinguishable. That suited his mood. He climbed up to the very top and for the first time, let himself in to his own front door. He was greeted by a sparse, damp room with a small, cracked window at the far end. One of the little panes was missing. It was cold and wallpaper was peeling everywhere, but there was a fireplace and a still serviceable Victorian button back chair. He walked into the kitchen and turned the stiff tap until it ran. He registered a table, an upright chair and a little oven. In the bedroom, there was an iron bedstead, a mattress and a mirror hanging on the wall by the door. He sat on the bed and was suddenly overcome with a tiredness so profound that he could not deny it. He swung his legs up onto the bed and went straight to sleep just as he was in his clothes and his boots.

Twelve hours later after a dreamless sleep, Simon woke up. He rubbed his eyes, looked at the ceiling and remembered sitting down on the bed and then nothing more. However, he realised that he was now warm and covered with blankets, although he had absolutely no memory of covering himself. He must have been exhausted, he thought because obviously he had done it during the night. Subconscious instincts were not something to be encouraged, but in this instance they seemed to have done no harm, so he dismissed this from his mind just as he'd done with so many other memories, and he went about his day.

Later on, he went out of the flat to buy provisions and firewood. His encounter with the outside world happened just as he wished: unnoticed he had slipped out of the building, and, loaded with what he needed, unnoticed he slipped back in. Having left the wood and kindling by the fireplace and his string bag in the kitchen, he allowed himself to feel rather pleased as he put his jacket over the back of the chair and went back into the sitting room. He sensed something different, something out of kilter. It wasn't as cold as he was expecting it to be, that was it. In fact now he thought about it, it wasn't as cold as it had been when he'd arrived yesterday. There was no draught.

To his surprise, when he looked at the window, he realised that the gap where a pane of glass was missing had been stuffed with newspaper. Taking the newspaper out of the frame, he saw that it had that day's date.

Someone had done this when he was out. No one else had a key, the lawyer had told him. No one could get in. Someone was intruding here. He had thought he was going to be able, in as much as it was possible, to have a kind of non-existence whilst still being alive. He recognised that he had been given a very special gift: the chance to live in a town and a building where nobody knew him and where he would have no financial burden. He would be forgotten by society and if he ever was to re-enter it and to rebuild himself, he could do it in his own time and by his own rules.

So now, on seeing the newspaper and its date, he wasn't frightened, he wouldn't allow himself to have the imagination to be frightened, but he was annoyed. This was a disruption and something of a mystery and he didn't want either.

However, there was no denying the fact that the room was more comfortable with the paper stuffed into the window, so he put it back, retreated into the kitchen and made himself a cup of tea. When his fingers closed round the warm cup his thoughts turned to the sea. Now he allowed himself to remember how curious he'd been about it when he had come here before. Perhaps in time, he might even try his hand at fishing. He had the very beginning of a plan. Moreover, as if observing himself from a distance, he was able to congratulate himself on the fact that finding the newspaper in the window pane did not seem to have seriously interrupted his equilibrium at all.

Lost in his thoughts, it took him sometime to become aware of a noise in the sitting room. Knocking the chair over in his haste, he rushed in and stopped short. At first the room seemed empty and untouched, but then he noticed a fire was being built in the grate. The kindling had been laid and one log was already in place.

Simon exploded, "Leave me alone. Don't do this, just go away." He punched the wall hard, bruising his knuckles in the process. "I can do this, I don't need anything, I don't need you, whoever you are. Piss off."

What would have been terrifying to other

people, was a rude and dangerous intrusion to him. He was frightened now, but not of whoever or whatever was doing this, he was frightened that something might jolt him out of his comfortable numbness and that scared him.

But, just as the paper had been useful in killing the draught, a fire was also needed to heat the room and he had to admit that he had bought the wood for that very purpose. It would be good to light it. So, when he had calmed down, when nothing else seemed to be happening, that is exactly what he did and he felt his anger leave him. He sat by the fire and taking out his pocket knife, began, for the first time in a long while, to whittle a piece of wood.

Eventually, Simon grew tired and the fire died down. Although he was reluctant to admit it, he felt more at peace that he had for a long time. Something had shifted inside him, but it didn't seem to be bad as he had feared it would be. It was time for bed, he'd had a full day.

He went into the bedroom and took off

his clothes. Standing in front of the mirror he examined his twisted and burnt leg which had mended into a tortuous shape. The sight no longer had the power to remind him of how it had happened, and when he looked up he saw that his face had lost its habitual grimace.

And then he began to smell the old, unmistakable smell of Yardley's Lavender Water. Behind him in the mirror he could make out the indistinct figure of a woman. She seemed to be smiling at him.

Acknowledgements

I am particularly grateful to the Ghost Book team who worked incredibly hard to produce this, especially Alexandra Mckellar, Bridget Whelan, Jenny Fraser-Smith and Jill Vigus. Without them, it would never have happened. I would also like to thank Volunteer Coordinator Gilly Burton, General Manager Phil Blume, Editor Peter Smith and the extraordinary team of volunteers past and present at The Regency Town House.

About the Author

Catherine Page worked in television drama at the BBC in the 1970s, then acted as a general amanuensis to her husband, a writer going blind, whilst bringing up her sons near Lisbon and then in Rome. The family came back to England in 2000, settled in Brighton, and after her husband's death, Catherine went back to University and completed two MAs.

Having been introduced to The Regency Town House in 2011, she has written street histories, guided tours, staffed the stall in the North Laine during the Brighton & Hove Open Door weekend, cleaned old layers of paint from the plaster in the hall, and played the part of Mrs Hankey who, with her husband Thomson, was the proud resident of Number 10 Brunswick Square for 30 years in the mid 19th century. Writing these ghost stories has been her first venture into the realms of fiction.

About the Illustrator

Jill Vigus is an artist/printmaker based in Brighton. Jill works in a variety of print media to make images that convey emotional messages of mystery and ambiguity. She uses a variety of printmaking methods, photopolymer etching, monotype, screen printing and often a mixture of all three making layered marks mixed with drawing, photographic stencils and lettering. Jill is interested in people and the places they occupy particularly those lost in the mists of time.

In 2016 she completed an MA in Sequential

Design/Illustration at the University of Brighton and added the making of artist books and zines to her practice which continues to evolve.

Jill has exhibited extensively and has work in private and public collections in the UK and abroad.

About The Regency Town House

The Regency Town House at 13 Brunswick Square, is a grade 1 listed terraced home in the heart of Brunswick Town, a Georgian estate in the City of Brighton and Hove on the Sussex coast.

Built in the 1820s, the Town House is being developed by staff and volunteers as a heritage centre and museum. Its activities are funded through The Brunswick Town Charitable Trust, a registered charity set up to support the project in 1994.

For more information please visit: www.rth.org.uk

Printed in Great Britain
by Amazon

70363832R00078